Friends Forever!

adapted by Natalie Shaw

poses and layouts by Jason Fruchter

Ready-to-Read

Simon Spotlight

New York London Toronto Sydney New Delhi

SIMON SPOTLIGHT
An imprint of Simon & Schuster Children's Publishing Division
1230 Avenue of the Americas, New York, New York 10020
This Simon Spotlight edition August 2022
© 2022 The Fred Rogers Company

For information about special discounts for bulk purchases, please contact
Simon & Schuster Special Sales at 1-866-506-1949 or business@simonandschuster.com.
Manufactured in the United States of America 0722 LAK
2 4 6 8 10 9 7 5 3 1
ISBN 978-1-5344-9897-6 (hc)
ISBN 978-1-5344-9896-9 (pbk)
ISBN 978-1-5344-9898-3 (ebook)

Daniel Tiger is
at school.

He asks Prince Wednesday, "Do you want to race with me?"

"Prince Wednesday is playing with Jodi. He is too busy to race cars," Daniel says.

Teacher Harriet sings, ♪ "Even when friends play with someone new, they will still be friends with you." ♪ ♪

Prince Wednesday will race his piggie! Jodi will race her moving truck!

They have so much
fun racing that they play
for a long time.

Then Jodi and Daniel pretend they are moving to a new house.

"I am playing with Jodi now, but I can play with you after," says Daniel.

Daniel has an idea and says, "We need books for our new house too."